W9-APH-744

CITY of SPIES

Thanks, in order of appearance, to our agents Victoria Sanders, Bernadette Baker and Gretchen Stelter; Mark Siegel, Tanya McKinnon, Calista Brill, Gina Gagliano, Colleen Venable and the rest of the First Second gang; and a special thanks to our collaborator, Pascal Dizin, whose prodigious talent and professionalism made this project a joy. —Susan Kim & Laurence Klavan

For all their advice, support, and just generally being great, my sincerest thanks to: David Mazzucchelli, Jason Little, Jessica Abel, Matt Madden, everyone at First Second, Susan and Laurence, Hilary Sycamore, Bob Mecoy, all my friends in the 2007-2008 SVA Cartooning Studio, and of course, my Mom. —Pascal Dizin

First Second
New York & London

Text Copyright © 2010 by Susan Kim & Laurence Klavan
Illustrations Copyright © 2010 by Pascal Dizin

Published by First Second
First Second is an imprint of Roaring Brook Press, a division of Holtzbrinck Publishing Holdings Limited Partnership, 175 Fifth Avenue, New York, NY 10010

All rights reserved

Distributed in Canada by H. B. Fenn and Company Ltd. distributed in the United Kingdom by Macmillan Children's Books, a division of Pan Macmillan.

Design by Colleen AF Venable
Colored by Hilary Sycamore and Sky Blue Ink

Cataloging-in-Publication Data is on file at the Library of Congress.
ISBN: 978-1-59643-262-8

First Second books are available for special promotions and premiums.
For details, contact: Director of Special Markets, Holtzbrinck Publishers.

First Edition May 2010
Printed in September 2009 in China by C&C Joint Printing Co., Shenzen, Guangdong Province
1 3 5 7 9 10 8 6 4 2

CITY of SPIES

Written by Susan Kim & Laurence Klavan
Illustrated by Pascal Dizin
Color by Hilary Sycamore

First Second
New York & London

WIND HOLDING STEADY... STANDING BY TO BEGIN DESCENT...

TAKE IT SLOW, SCHULTZ... VE WANT THOSE PHOTOGRAPHERS DOWN THERE TO GET A GOOD LOOK AT THE GERMAN MIRACLE, NEIN?

GET THE CHAMPAGNE READY... WE ARE ABOUT TO MAKE HISTORY!
HINDENBURG

GOLLY, ZIRCONIUM MAN—
—THAT'S THE HINDENBURG! DIDN'T IT BURN UP YEARS AGO?
IT SURE DID, SCOOTER. BUT THANKS TO MY TIME TRAVEL MACHINE, WE CAN GO BACK FIVE YEARS TO 1937 AND KEEP IT FROM HAPPENING. OTHERWISE, DOZENS OF PEOPLE WILL DIE!
TIME TRAVEL MACHINE

HURRY... NO TIME FOR SIGHTSEEING!

NAVIGATION

WATCH IT, SCOOTER!

WHA-?

BUT WHAT IS IT?
I DON'T KNOW. BUT WE'D BETTER GET UP THERE BEFORE IT DOES!

JUST MAKE SURE IT DOESN'T TOUCH YOU!

ONCE THOSE FLAMES HIT THE HYDROGEN SUPPLY... THERE'S NO STOPPING IT!

ZIRCONIUM MAN-

BEHIND YOU!

HEY, SCOOTER... THINK THOSE DODGERS HAVE A SHOT AT THE PENNANT?

WINK!

BOF!

POP!
SPRAY!

FIZZLE...

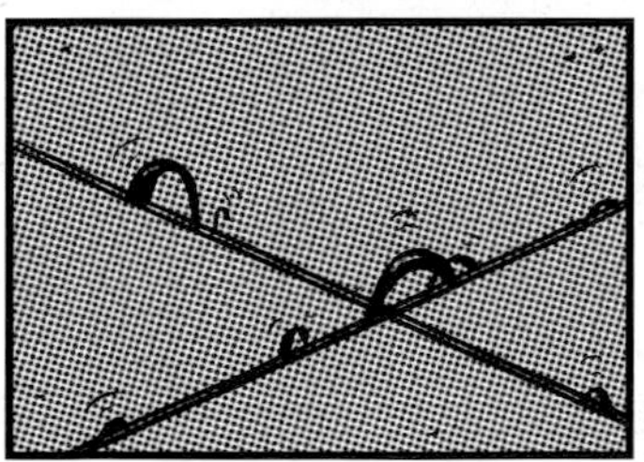

Time to quit daydreaming, kiddo...

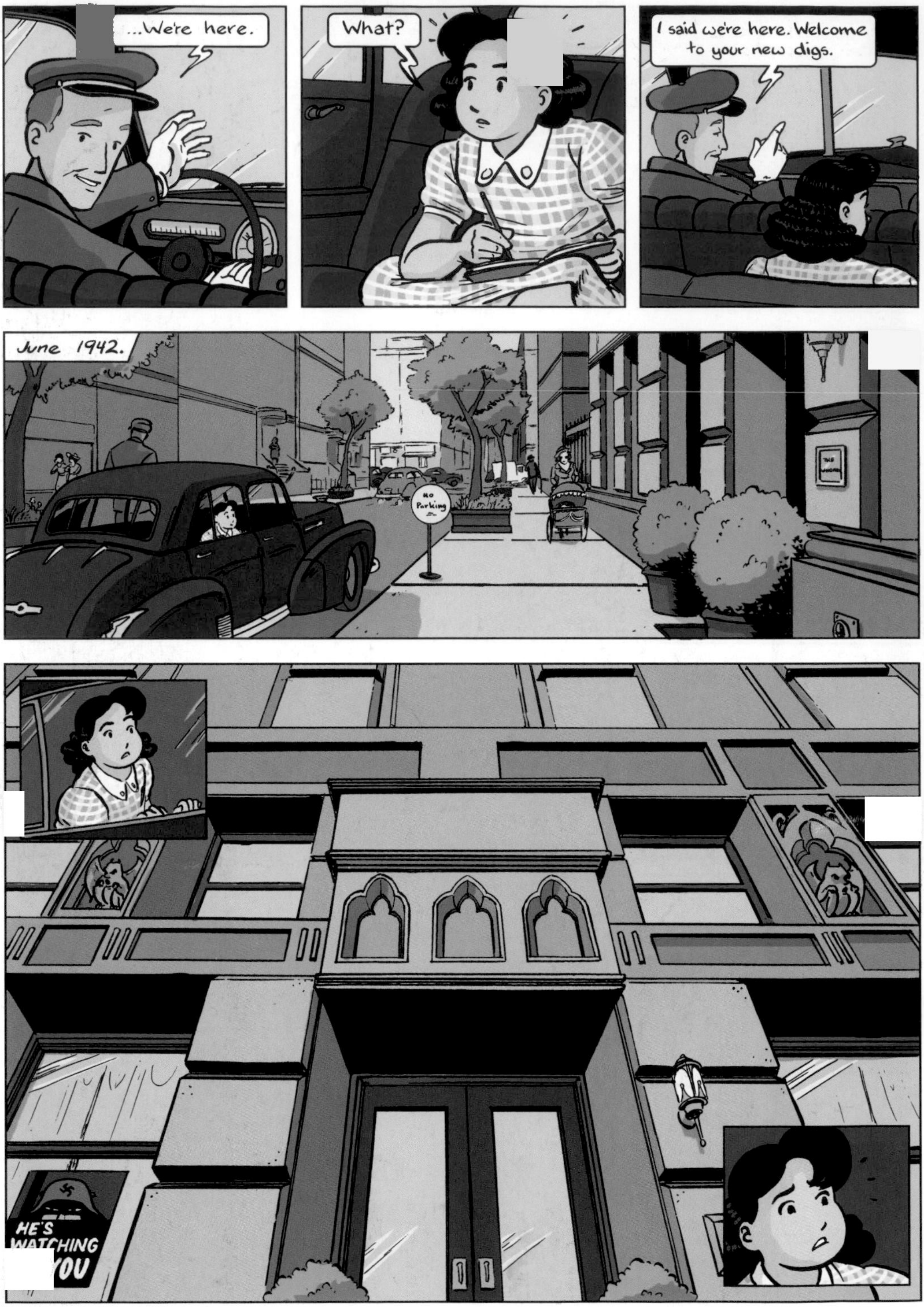

HE'S WATCHING YOU

I'm surprised no one's down to meetcha.
Hey, hey... vat do you think you're doing?
No Parking

GASP!

I'm dropping the kid off. She's spending the summer with her aunt.
I know nothing of such plans! Vat kid? Who is this aunt? *Stop that immediately!*

Hallo... Miss Spiegelman? This is—

I cannot allow this. You have no aussorization!

Look, pal... you don't got any choice.

Her dad's getting hitched again. Funny thing. He keeps getting older, the wives stay the same age.

Anyway, he don't want her back until September. And he usually gets what he wants.
But you have no right... I have orders...!

What a sweet little girl!

Ahh!
BUMP!

...oww!

BING!

WHRRRRRR...

3
2
L
B
BING!

CRRRRR...

Yahhhhhh!
EEEEEEEKK!

SLAM!
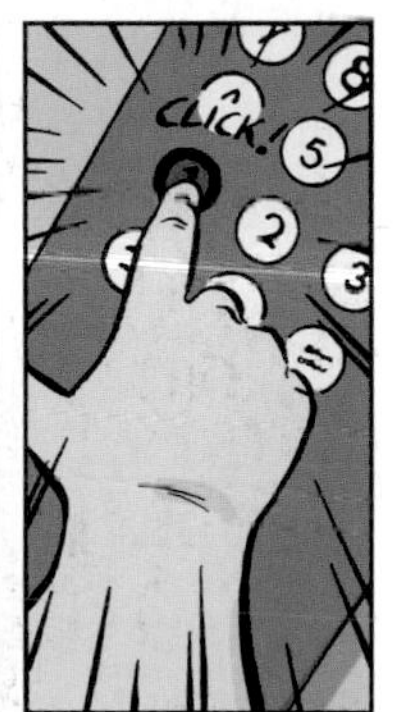
CLICK!

?

KNOCK!
KNOCK!

Miss Spiegelman?

Miss Spiegelman!
Oh, rats... it wasn't today, was it?

You must be Evelyn.

CURTSY

Here, Karl...
you're a peach.

Okay, guys... that's enough for today. Am-scray already!

?

Excuse me...
Aunt Lia?

Aunt Lia?

What? Oh... you mean me! God, "Aunt Lia"... *that's* bizarre.

Excuse me, but... where's my room?
Oh.

Well, just pick one. Try the fourth one on the left.

CLICK

SIGH...

TAP TAP

So... first trip to New York, huh? Anything you're just dying to do?

Well...

My dad's taking me to a Dodgers game on the Fourth of July. But maybe we could see one before then...?

SNORT!

I hate sports. But tell you what— how about world religion? There's a symposium on the Dalai Lama next week.

And a Picasso show at the Matisse Gallery that I'm just dying to see... want another herring?

Sob...!

SNIFF!

SNIFF.
ZIRCONIUM MAN

Hey... whatcha doing there, chief?
WHUMP!

Nothing.
Look, sugar, I know this is new for both of us, and, uh... I was thinking.

There are at least a dozen young people in the building. How about I throw you a party tomorrow night and invite some of them up?

Really? You mean a party... for me?
Sure! Does that sound okay?

It sure does. Thank you, Aunt Lia — that sounds swell!

Plant you now, dig you later...

Means "au revoir"!..

...But that's just it! They all have the same names, and they all sound alike... how can anyone tell who's a spy and who's not?
You're talking about Americans who happen to be German. It's not their fault what's going on in Germany.
You mean those awful rumors about what's happening to the Jews?

All I can say is, I'm doing my part for Uncle Sam. I'm air raid warden for the building.

Watch out, sister... loose lips sink ships!

BANG!

HA HA HA HA HA HA

HA, HA...
SCOOTER!

HA HA
SCOOTER!

TAKE ME OUT TO THE–
OOTER!

♪ -BALL GAME ♫
TAKE ME OUT WITH THE CROWD! ♫
♪ BUY ME SOME PEANUTS AND CRACKER JACK... ♫
EBBETS FIELD
OT DOGS
AND NOW, TO COMMEMORATE HIS SAVING THE HINDENBURG FROM EXPLODING MIDAIR INTO A MILLION PIECES — OH, THE HUMANITY, IF THAT HAD ACTUALLY HAPPENED!—

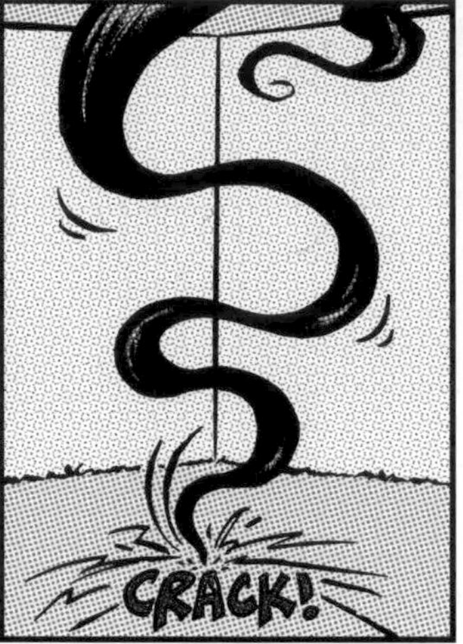

CRACK!

TOSS!

YAAAAAAAAAAAAAA-

SHOOP!

ZIRCONIUM MAN! LOOK!

AAAAAAAAAAAAAAAAH!!!

WE'RE SURROUNDED... WHAT DO WE DO NOW?

DON'T YOU THINK WE SHOULD SHED A LITTLE LIGHT ON THE SITUATION?
?

—WINK!

CLICK!

ZAP!
ZOT!
SIZZLE!
SCREEEEEE!!

EEEEEEEEEEEEEEEEEEEEEEEEEEEEE

LOOK... IT'S ZIRCONIUM MAN AND SCOOTER!
THEY SAVED US... AGAIN!

HURRAY FOR ZIRCONIUM MAN AND SCOOTER! HURRAY!
DODGERS
DODGERS
DODGERS
DODGERS
DODGERS

MR. PRESIDENT!

Excuse me... mind if I go into the bathroom?

What?!

There's a leak downstairs. Mind if we take a look at your bathroom?
Oh. Sure, go ahead.

Geez. I guess some folks don't know there's a war going on, huh, Tony? Pass me the wrench, wouldja?

Uh... here ya go.

Well... you're getting better. *sigh...* I'll be right back.

TAP! TAP!

So, you're staying here with your aunt, huh? My pop says she's spoiled rotten.
She is not!

BANG!

HA HA, HA, HA, HA!
...Well, maybe a little...

Then I betcha you're spoiled rotten too. 'Cause you're rich.

And that's not all. You're German, right?
I'm American— the same as you!

I mean your family's a bunch of Krauts.
I'm Jewish, you idiot!

So what? I bet you're a Nazi... 'cause my uncle says all Germans are Nazis.

Nazi spy! Nazi spy!
Shut up! I am not!
SHOVE!

GRAPPLE!

SPLASH!

My notebook!!

SPLISH!
SPLASH!

It ain't so bad. Look... I think I can fix it...

Isn't it going to catch fire?

Hope not. My pop'll kill me.

ZIRCONIUM MAN AND SCOOTER

Here. Good as new. Kinda.

GRAB!
FLIP, FLIP, FLIP!

So. Where'd you get it?
I did it.

You're kidding. My pop won't even let me read comics. You mean you drew the pictures and everything?

See? This is Zirconium Man. He's a superhero.

So who's this? She looks like you.
That's Scooter. She's his helper. Whenever he mentions the Dodgers, that's her cue.

Wow! Her shoe hits the bad guy right in the head!
BAM!

I want to be a hero, too. Maybe not yet. But one day.

Swell. And I thought this was going to be a boring summer. I'm the only kid in the building.
What about that other boy? That big meanie who tried to scare me when I moved in? He was a real creep.

Oh. Well. That was me.

I didn't know it was you, okay? I thought it was Karl.

...you mean the doorman?

HA HA HA HA!
Talk about a big meanie!

Yeah! — So I get even with him every chance I get. One time, I put itching powder in his sweater.
HA HA HA!

Another time, I put ants in his locker, and—
HA
HA
HA
HA

Tony! Is that you down there?
LAUNDRY
GIGGLE!

Coming, Pop!

LAUNDRY

Are you living with your aunt for keeps?
No... just for the summer.

What about your folks?

My mother died when I was little. My dad's been married five or six times since then.
Really? You mean you have more than one mom?

Sure.

Wow! What's that like?

Well...

The new one looks exactly like Lana Turner. And the one before that looked like Ginger Rogers. And the one before that looked like Veronica Lake... and the one before that looked like...

Tony!

It's cold out here, you're gonna catch your death...

Hey Evelyn... wait up!

You ever been to German Town before?
What's that?

We're in it, dope. That's this whole neighborhood.

If you want, I can show you around tomorrow.

That sounds great!

See you tomorrow. I mean— plant you now... dig you later!

SOB!

...German spies in a U-boat off the coast of Long Island. Citizens are urged to report any suspicious activity to the authorities...

BLEH...

Uhh... hello? Excuse me?

...Fred? Would you like some coffee?
It's Bob. And no thanks.

mmm...

'Bye, Aunt Lia!

All right — no, I mean it's not all right. I mean... shouldn't you have a... you know. A nanny or a nurse or something?

Oh, no. I'm way too old for that.

But what about—

SLAM!

Doesn't anyone want any coffee?

You mean to tell me, you never been on a bus before?

USA MEATS
UNCLE SAM DONUT SHOP
RED WHITE 'N' BLUE SHOE REPAIR
149 UNCLE SAM DONUT SHOP
USA MEATS BRATWURST LIVERWURST
HOT COFFEE

What do you mean? They all sound American to me.

Yeah, dope. 'Cause they're owned by Germans and we're at war with Germany, remember?

What's in there?

"American National Socialist Headquarters."
AMERICAN NATIONAL SOCIALIST HEADQUARTERS

Tony... there's Nazis in there!

Well, there used to be a lot of them around here. The Bund. Silver Shirts. They got the heck out when the war started.

Or so they say...

PASTRY SHOP
YANKEE DOODLE
PASTRY SHOP
PULL FOR STOP

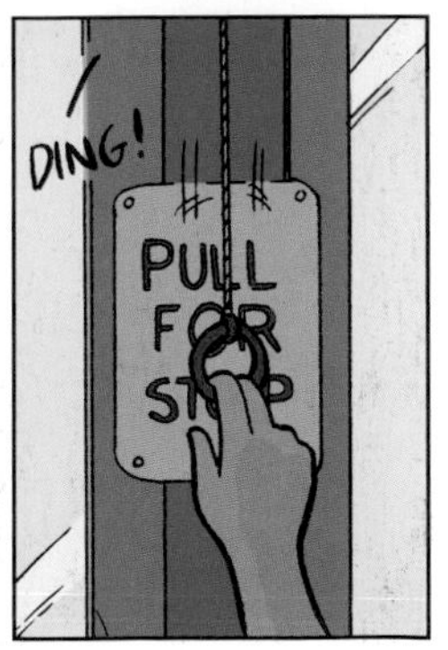
DING!

So vat can I get for you, Liebchen?
TOUSLE!
MATCHES FREE

Look, Snaps, I tried with that—spy—last week.
You mean the jaywalker?

He was acting suspiciously!

Or the purse snatcher you thought was a spy? Or the nut job on Lexington you thought was a spy? Or the—

Hey, flatfoot!

... pass the milk.
You wanna go downtown? Do you?!

Easy there, Seabiscuit.

He's really got flat feet, see. 4F.

Oops. Sorry.

NUM!
MMM!
MMM!
CHEW!

Urrrgh...

WHOOOOO

OOOOOOOOOO
Air raid, darling! Close the blackout curtains and meet me downstairs!

OOOOOOOOOOOOOOOOOOOOOo...
EXIT

Psst... Evelyn!

Up here!
ROOF ACCESS

What are you doing? The Nazis are attacking!

Awww... it's only a drill and nothin' good ever happens anyway.

Come on!
ROOF

But we're gonna get in trouble!
Scaredy-cat!

Pow! Pow pow pow! Know what I wish? I wish I was a fighter pilot like my Uncle Sal.

Yeah... me too!
TWIRL!

Hey, Tony — look who's down there!

So? It's your aunt. And that fat lady from 46.
No — they're Nazi paratroopers.

Huh?
Stay right here.

RUSTLE, RUSTLE!

What are you doing?
You'll see.

Eleven minutes forty one seconds! Not as good as last time. We—

SPLASH!

What was that?

SPLOOSH!

...it's a bomb!

Don't be silly. It's only a—
BANG!
SPLASH!

Help! We're being attacked!

Take that, you stupid Nazi!

Wow... right on his head!
See if I can get that other one. Hey, Nazi... here it comes...!

SPLOOSH!

HA HA HA
HA HA HA HA

...urk?
YANK!

...we were pretending to bomb Nazis.

So. You want to be a hero, is that it?

Being a hero isn't about playing games and pretending. It's a real thing — being brave... and standing up for what's right. That's what I saw in the Battle of the Marne.

You understand?
...yes, sir.

And Miss Spiegelman... not that it's any of my business...

But even in the best gardens, tomatoes need a little support to grow right.

THE THREE STOOGES
IN
You Nazty Spy!

You see, anyone can be brave. Like Moe, look at him.

Excuse me.

SHHH
... Is this all you got?

I betcha got more. Where you keep your money, in your training bra?

HAW HAW HAW
SHOVE!

Hey... lookit me-

I got four eyes!
HAW
HAW

-stop picking on her!

What did you say?

GULP! ... y-you heard.

I said, give her back her glasses!
Who's gonna make us?

SHOVE!

SHOVE!

C'mon. Let's leave the babies alone.
TOSS!

"The hunt for Nazi spies continues across the nation!"

"With the suspicious sinking of the Normandie in New York last February... what else does Herr Hitler have up his sleeve? Citizens of New York City are being asked by your Federal Bureau of Investigation to keep an eye out for suspicious behavior."

I WANT TO THANK YOU, ZIRCONIUM MAN AND SCOOTER...
F.B.I.
J. EDGAR HOOVER

...FOR YOUR WONDERFUL WORK IN FIGHTING EVIL.
AIDE
CLIP!
FLASH!
FLASH!

AIDE

AND NOW...

...THIS IS TOP SECRET. THERE ARE NAZI SPIES LOOSE IN GERMAN TOWN. A WHOLE NEST OF THEM!

NOW THAT THEY FINISHED WITH THE NORMANDIE, THEY'RE PLANNING TO BLOW UP TIMES SQUARE ON JULY FOURTH.
HOLY COW!

LOOKS LIKE WE'VE GOT OUR JOB CUT OUT FOR US!
RIGHT. THIS IS BIG. THIS IS ABOUT SAVING OUR COUNTRY.

Hey, look, I can touch my nose with my tongue!

See?

There's no time to goof around now... this is serious!

THE ENEMY IS LISTENING

HE'S WATCHING YOU
THE ENEMY IS LISTENING
THE ENEMY IS LISTENING

What do you think? Is he a spy?
Don't think so.

What about him?
Not clear.

Oh, now, he's gotta be!

Uh-uh. No cuffs.

Yeah. So?
Straight legs are American-style. Dope.

Hey, that's really smart. We need someone with a German accent.

TICK...

Tony!
PUUR!

Don't worry... it's invisible ink. It'll fade in fifteen minutes.
INVISIBLE INK

BING!

Right on time! Quick... come on!

CLIP

Aggghhh!

GIGGLE!

Vat were you doing in my locker?! Did you touch anything in there?
No. Look... it's already fading! Just don't heat it up, okay?

Don't you ever go near it again! You hear me? Don't you ever!

Schweinhunden! Ich habe keine Zeit für so etwas!

Verdammter Unruhestifter!
TICK, TICK

SLAM!
TICK, TICK, TICK...

Geez. Did you really hear it ticking?
Didn't you?

He sure is acting sneaky, ain't he?

Hello? *Ja*, it's me. I got something for you. Something I think you're gonna like.
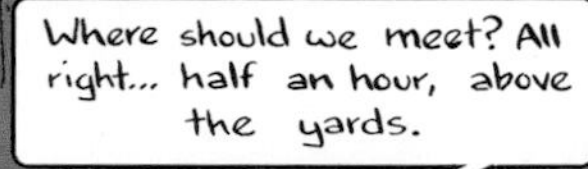
Where should we meet? All right... half an hour, above the yards.

Ja, gut. Bis bald. Seien Sie nicht spät.

Did you hear that? He's going to the yards.

... like the Brooklyn **navy** yards?

You mean... where the ships are?

This is too big for us. We've got to report this to somebody!

YANKEE DOODLE
PASTRY SHOP
KILROY WAS HERE

SIGH...

Hey, Rembrandt — time to put down the brush!
TAP TAP!

HEH...
PLUNK!

Here. It's chicken salad today.
My favorite. Thanks, Brendan.

Officer? Officer!

—you've gotta help us!
There's this Nazi spy and he's got a bomb and he's getting away!

Here we go again.

Whoa, whoa, back up... what are you saying?

It's the doorman of our building. We know he's a spy 'cause he has cuffed pants, and talks with an accent, and he's acting really funny!

Acting funny? You look around, kiddo? You're in Manhattan.
HA...

We're serious! He has this wrapped package... and it's ticking!

Listen, you two... you've been watching too many movies.

But we heard him say he was gonna deliver the goods... to the Brooklyn Navy Yards!

He went down Lexington and... look!
POLICE

That's him!

Stay here.

THE YARDS
BAR
BAR · GRILL
ROOMS TO LET

A Caucasian male came in here with a package. Do you know what room he went to?

Maybe. My memory's not what it used to be.
LIFE

307
KNOCK
KNOCK
KNOCK!

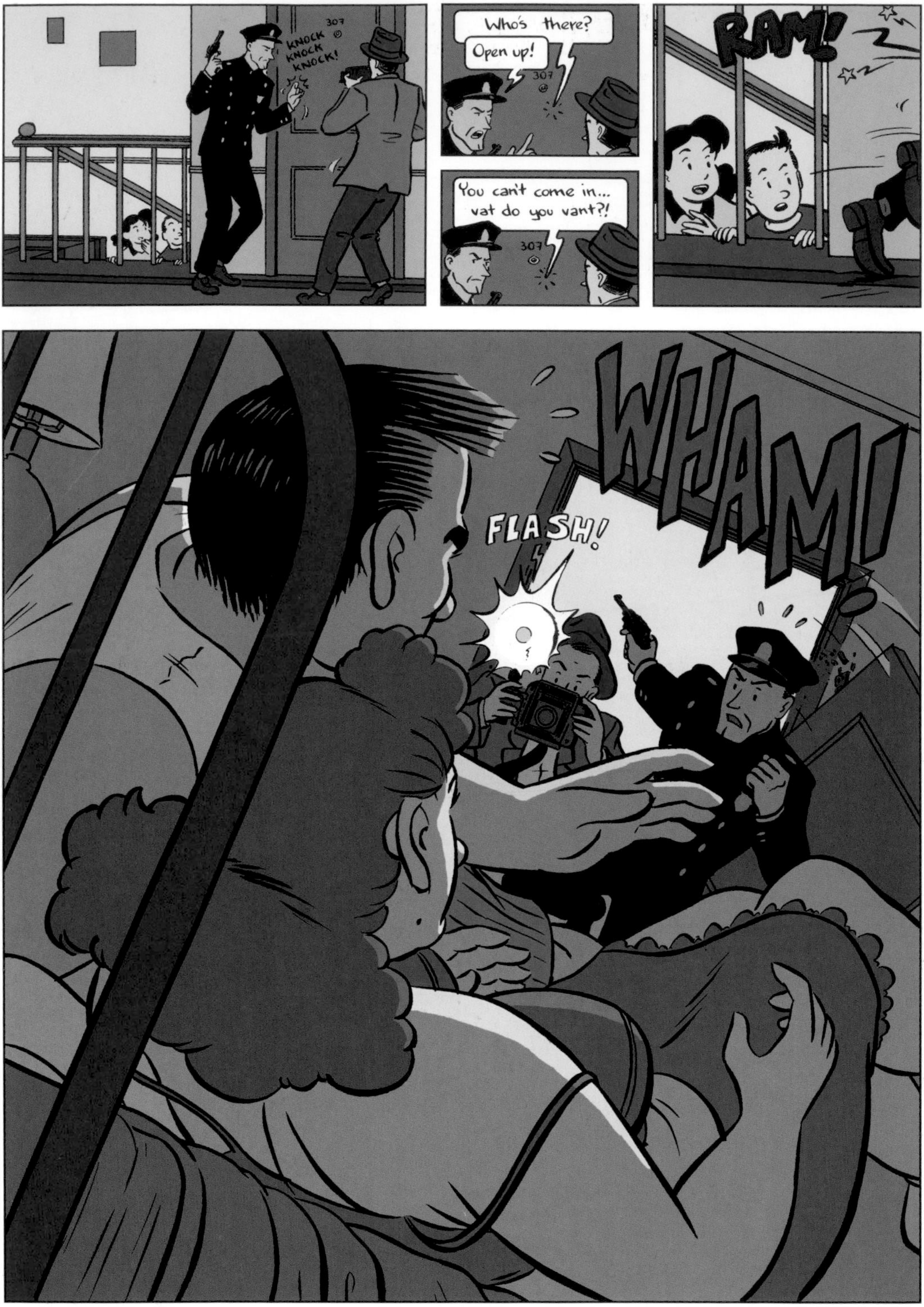

Who's there?
Open up!
307

You can't come in... vat do you vant?!
307

RAM!

WHAM!

FLASH!

AIIIEEEE!!

FLASH!

Vat is going on?! Vat is the meaning of this?!

FLASH!

You two!!
FLASH!

Uh-oh.

TICK.

TICK.

TICK!

CUCKOO!
CUCKOO!
CUCKOO!

The Daily Gazette

HE'S CHEATING, NOT SPYING!

BUY MORE WAR BONDS

FALSE SPY REPORTS TRIPLE- NOW IT'S EVEN LITTLE GIRLS!

NAZIS ON THE MOVE IN EUROPE

Read all about it!

Brendan Hughes of the 19th Precinct, Ma'am.
Why... you're the policeman from the paper!

That's right, now, look... I need to see your daughter and—

You mean my niece.

Right! I need for her to... come downtown with me.

Whatever for?

I need her to, well... to talk to my captain. To, you know, tell him why I... to explain what—
You mean... to "take the fall"?

Uh...

You ought to be ashamed of yourself. A grown man, trying to blame a little girl for your own—
Look, it's not like that, I—

If you hadn't gone off half-cocked in the first place... any idiot could've told you nothing was going on—

Hey, in case you haven't noticed, we're at war—

Oh, really? Thanks for the headline!
—not that you care about anything going on outside your penthouse.

You and all your crazy... *hooey*—

I'm sorry... it's called abstract art, ever heard of it?

You mean, when they call a picture "Portrait of Gladys" and what it really looks like is a fur hat that somebody sat on?

And speaking of which...

Good day, officer!

SNAP!

ERRRRT!

Evelyn? Honey? There's someone here to see you.

Daddy!

HUG!

There I was, thinking I had a daughter who could behave herself, so I could go on my honeymoon without any problems. You really let me down this time, Scooter.

Daddy, I-

Am I going to have to cancel my plans just to keep an eye on you? Is that what you want? Lenora will be very disappointed.

No, don't do that, I-

Well? What do you think I should do?

... I'd like to stay here.

How do I know you won't go humiliating me again? Because you have made me the laughingstock of Westport.

I'm sorry, Daddy. I was only trying to help...

Look... we'll let this one go.

Just remember, I expect a clean report when I see you again in September.

September? But... what about the Fourth of July?

The what?

You said we could go to a Dodgers game. You said we could sit in a box and eat Cracker Jack...

Daddy, you *promised*...
...Oh. Yes. Well, obviously, that's no longer the plan, I'll be on the Amalfi coast. But here.

Glad you reminded me. I was all set to throw it in the trash... but you might as well have it.

You can't act like a kid forever, Lia. I mean, just look at you. Are you going to be a screw-up your entire life?
Now, Spence, that's not entirely fair, I—
CLICK.

You can hardly take care of yourself, much less a ten-year-old. Should I put her somewhere else? I can hire someone to take care of her...
I can handle it! I'm not such an idiot, you know... I'm a lot more competent than you think...

Okay. Then for starters, I expect her to be a little more selective as to playmates.

You mean Tony? He's a good kid, Spence, I really don't think we have to...

Stop being so soft, Lia. It's time to suck it up.

SLAM!

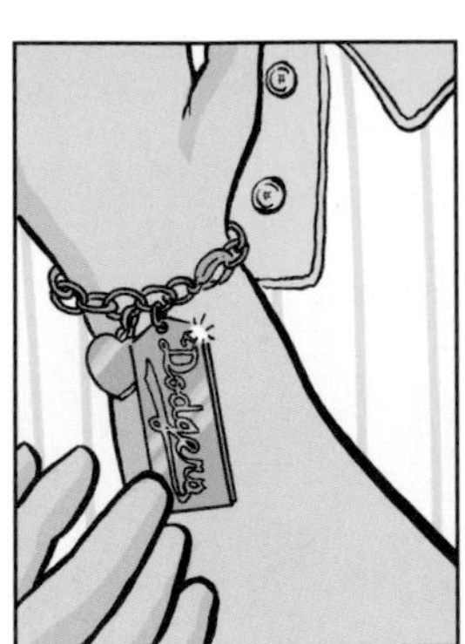
Dodgers

Hey... so they let you out! Mom? Dad? Is it okay if Evelyn comes in?

No, I...

NOD

I just came down here to say... I can't play with you anymore.

...What?

I've got to suck it up. I'm sorry.

SKUNCH!

ZIRCONIUM MAN AND SCOOTER

COLUMBIA UNIVERS
SOUTH FIELD STADIUM
GO LIONS!
GO LION

ENTRY

NO
ENTRY.
CLICK!

Working late again, Dr. Johnson?
Just some research to finish up.

CLICK!

CLASSIFIED

TOP SECRET
SNAP!

FO Y-SECOND ST
TIMES SQ

CHEVROLET
PLANTERS
PEANUTS
A BAG A DAY
FOR MORE PEP
THE PAUSE THAT REFRESHES

AUTOMAT
DESSERTS

Is that the last butterscotch pudding?

Here. You take it.

THE TIMES

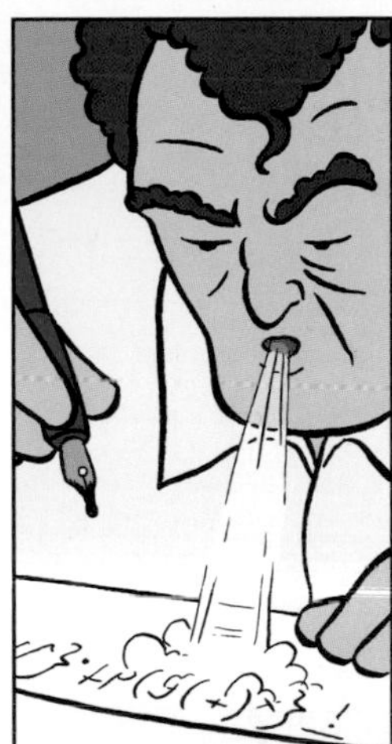

{x(t)f) dt.

Wolfgang! Dinner!
Be right there!

Rats!

?

ZIRCONIUM MAN AND SCOOTER

I'm sure glad Zirconium Man got out of that scrape. Thank God for that Scooter, huh?

I threw that away. It's junk.

I guess artistic talent must run in the family.
CAPTAIN MARVEL

First your mother, then me... and now you.

... my mother?

Wow... she was good!

What's this... tent thingamajig?

It's a hoopa. Or a chuppah, whatever they call it.

We weren't raised with much religion. I guess you weren't either.

So what happened to her drawing? Didn't she do it anymore?

No. After she and your Dad got married, Sookie just gave it up.

But why?

Who knows?

But one thing I do know is that you've got talent... just like me. And no matter what, we're not going to give up on it...

Promise?

Promise!

You can hold onto those, if you want.
PHOTOS

And here.
PAT PAT

Feel free to help yourself to any of my art stuff. There's paints, pastels, charcoals, you name it...
Wow... thanks, Aunt Lia!

Your father's right. It's time I did start taking myself more seriously.

"Shot down three... single-handedly captured... hailed as fearless..."

Beer
Jeez Louise!
Hey, there's the defender of democracy. How are things downtown, hero?

What? Well, I—

Here's a free beer for the G-man.
Thanks.

That'll be two bits, Flatfoot.

Sigh...

Don't worry.

Let me buy a beer for my baby brother.

♪ ...which nobody can deny! ♫

A doorman with a glad eye... and a little girl as your source.

You're lucky Mom and Dad aren't alive. Dad would have used his belt on you, I don't care how big you are.

Only if you snitched on me, as per usual.

Why don't you let us boys at the Bureau handle the war? There's nothing wrong with just catching crooks.

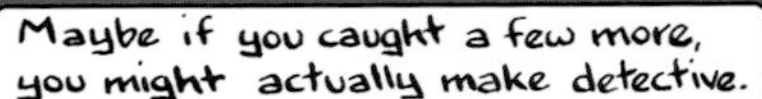
Maybe if you caught a few more, you might actually make detective.

I do just fine.
NUDGE, NUDGE

And this one's on me.

Sigh... You got a sawbuck?
Don't worry about it.

So long, flatfoot!

ALFIE'S BAR
ALFIE'S BAR

Sigh...

Riinnnngg...

Hey, Brendan! It's your brother!

Maybe I was a little hard on you tonight, Bren. Why don't you come up this weekend? Ginny'll make her famous pot pie, and I know that Ellie, Margaret, Benny, and the twins would love to see their Uncle Brendan.

And I can meet another one of those boring nurses or teachers you're always setting me up with?

Sorry, pal, but maybe the Amelia Earharts of the world would rather hang out with the Charles Lindberghs, you know what I mean?

Hey, for your information... I already got a good-looking broad wearing just her **hair** on my bed right now. I don't need your help, "FBI man"—with **anything**! And one day, maybe you're gonna need mine!

SLAM!

Stop looking at me that way.

ALL ABOARD THE FERRY FOR THE PICNIC!

HA, HA, HA, HA

ENGINE ROOM

ZIRCONIUM MAN! LOOK!
EEK!
AAAAH!

LOOK, SWEETHEART! WE'RE SAVED!

YAY! IT'S ZIRCONIUM MAN AND SCOOTER!

ENGINE
ROOM

CRASH!

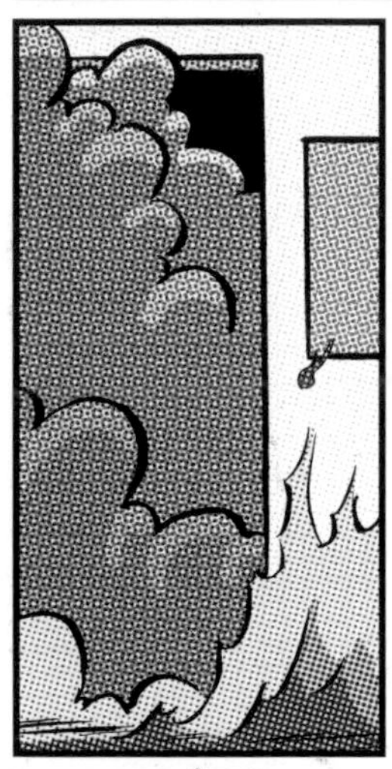

ZIRCONIUM?
ARE YOU IN THERE?

GOSH, YOU HAD ME
SCARED FOR A SECOND!

BANG!

BANG!

BANG!

BANG!
BANG!
BANG!

Can't talk. Gotta lotta work.
Oh, yeah? What's wrong?

Oh, you know... it's a... thingamabob that's... about to go on the fritz... it's pretty serious... BANG!
BANG!
BANG!

Really? Can I see?
It's right... there... next to the whatchamacallit, and I... BANG!
BANG!

BANG!

SPRRT!

EEEEEEEEEK!

HA... HA, HA, HA, HA, HA!

I told you it was broken!

Naww. Pop yelled and everything, but I heard him and my ma laughing about it later.

Hey — you ever play stickball?

No... is it fun?

I'll say! First, you get a stick. Then you get a ball. Then you... c'mon, let's go!

Ohh... it's no good. I can't go outside, remember?

Well, stay right here. I got a better idea!

HOUDINI

FINE GRADE CIGARS

DAREDEVIL
SENSATION COMICS
ALL WINNERS
ACTION COMICS

ACTION COMICS
CANDY

5 AND 10 CENT SHOP

Ooof!

Sorry, Mister, I was just—

PHEW!

Hey! Hey, Mister, you got my—

So much for my big plans. All because of some jerk! Pardon my French.

And you shoulda seen the guy when we knocked into each other. Like he was gonna kill me or something.

Like who wants his dumb ol' book, anyhow? And there was some mighty fine comics in that bag, and some jawbreakers, and wax lips, and...

I've, umm, *heard* of this book.
So what? Bet it's boring.

EDITH WOODWARD
Always Pamela
NO MAN COULD RESIST HER LOVE!
No, actually, I've heard it's kind of...

...interesting.

Really?

When you ride ALONE you ride with Hitler!

You know, Pascal... "when you ride alone, you ride with Hitler." Maybe I'd better walk.

Why don't you take the week off? Don't worry... I'll be fine.

Remi ART Gallery

He says he doesn't know the name.

Tell him he's a friend of my family's.

He says he still doesn't—
Mention there was a Christmas party at my apartment. Tell him I still have his suspenders.

Striped suspenders.

That's it — knock it off!
Hey... Brendan... It's just a gag... Take it easy...

You think you're so innocent? You think you're not a menace? You are!

Is it all the sandwiches? I promise—you don't hafta gimme 'em any more! I don't need 'em!

Next time I'll throw you in jail. And that'll be the end of you. *Capiche?*
NOD! NOD!

... SIGH...

SCREECH!

Hey, lady, whaddya think you're—

—oh, geez Louise. Not you again.
Wonderful. Are you going to arrest *me* now?

Well, you *were* jaywalking. That's a Section A-16, and—

Wait—Aunt Lia! Aunt Lia!
2V321
SCREECH!

Would you please keep your voice down?! And stop calling me that!

SIGH...

I'm sorry. *Thank you.* Now what do I owe you?
What?

Hey, what are you doing? I don't want your money... put that away! Jeez!

...I'm sorry. I didn't mean to—look, I just wanted to say thank you. Can I at least buy you a cup of coffee?

Mrs. Schmidt makes the best strudel in German Town. Sure you don't want any?
Oh no... I'm too excited to eat a thing.

I actually just had some wonderful news... I sold a painting to a very prestigious curator.

Wow... really? Must be nice to have everything cut your way. You got money, success... you don't even get killed crossing against the light.

It's a different story for the rest of us, believe me.

SOB!

Hey, it's okay... I'm used to it.

It's not that... I didn't sell anything! He wouldn't even see me... his receptionist took one look at my painting and she laughed! I threw it in the garbage. I... I've never sold anything... I'm not an artist, I'm a total fraud!

Hey. Here.

PHWEE!

What do they know anyway, right? Sounds like a bunch of jerks to me...

That's very gallant. In fact... it's nice just sitting here in the company of a full-bodied man.
SNIFF...

You mean on account of the war?
And on account of the men I usually hang around with.

Yeah, well. I'm not really full-bodied. I mean...

I got flat feet. 4-F. I was chasing a burglar — Three-Fingered Floyd?

—and I was jumping from one roof to another, twenty feet about —when I landed splat, on my dogs.
SMACK!

He got the paddy wagon. I got, you know, shoe pads.

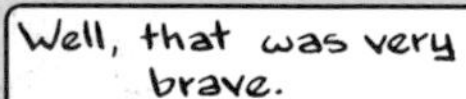

Well, that was very brave.

Nah. That's what they pay me for. It's not like what our boys are doing on Midway.

All I can do is act like an idiot and pinch that poor dope of a doorman...

You made a mistake.

Well, that *is* the way it works with leads. You never know.
Exactly. You never know.

See, all I ever wanted to do was help people, to be needed. Not for the awards and medals part of it, just...

Well, you've helped *someone* today.
Have I?

NOD

Hey... I wanted to give you this.

That's from my sculpture!
It kinda jumped off at me when I hung my hat on it. But—you mind if I hold onto it awhile? It's starting to grow on me.

Keep it. You might have a door that won't stay open.

Speaking of being needed, I'd better get going...

Y'know, they're right. This book really is... interesting.

Maybe I oughta get myself a library card.
Should we stop for now? Or maybe- one more chapter?

Yeah-one more chapter.

What's a "codpiece"?

...They're like fishsticks.
Oh. Got it.

Hey... that's weird.

I'll say.
No, I meant... did you notice that some of the letters are underlined?

What do you mean?

Look.

And on some of the other pages the corners are turned down, see?

I think it started a few chapters back.
FLIP,
FLIP!

See—there's an "A."

Oh, yeah. Willya look at that.

And look, here—there's an "L," and...

... another "A," and...
EDITH WOODWARD

ALH

So what's... "Al-ham-bra"?
?

...Okay, here we go. The *Alhambra*.

THE ALHAMB
You can't imagine what it looks like in person. It's like standing inside... the world's biggest Fabergé egg.
What are these?

Oh... those are the floor plans, see? Each of these dots is a column... those are doorways... those are windows, I guess...

So is there anything special about the Alhambra?
Well... it's the most glorious Moorish palace in Spain. Why do you want to know?

No reason. Is it okay if I borrow this?
... you can keep it.
Oh boy... thanks!

Oh—and thanks for all the toys and dolls and stuff. They're really neat, Aunt Lia!

KISS!

HA, HA, HA... CLINK, CLINK, HA...

HA HA

Could everybody please pipe down? Can't you see it's after nine?!

DIVE!

SPLASH!

ZIRCONIUM MAN!

BUT I CAN'T HELP YOU... I DON'T KNOW HOW, I'M JUST A KID!

YAAAAH!

QUICK, GRAB ON... AS TIGHT AS YOU CAN!

AIIIIEEEEEEE!!!!

SPLOOSH!
...mmm...

SNIP SNIP!

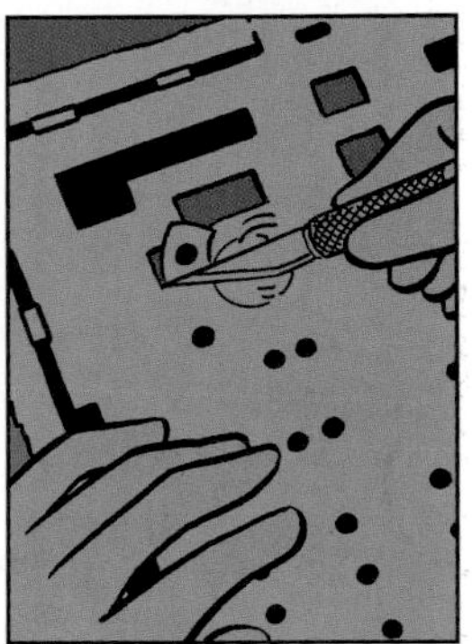

FLIP FLIP!

..."system of gaseous diffusion"...

"necessary to effect separation of the isotopes"...

"in order to achieve fission..."

... Yeah?
TONY'S ROOM

C'mon... we've got work to do!

5 AND 10 CENT SHOP
Are you sure this is a good idea?

Now who's being chicken?
I'm not being chicken, I'm just not sure it's gonna work, is all.

Why wouldn't it work?
A million reasons.

Her, for instance.

Oh, no! Don't do it, lady! Don't do it!

Shoo. That was close.

Besides. If he woulda come back, he woulda come back already.

I know. And if he came back once, he'll come back again.
How do you figure?

He made a big mistake taking the wrong bag, right?
CENT SHOP

So he's scared he's gonna get punished... maybe even bumped off.

So he's gonna keep coming back—hoping that somehow, somebody brought the *right* one back.

See?
Holy smoke.

CENT SHOP
GLANCE! GLANCE!

Let's go!

714

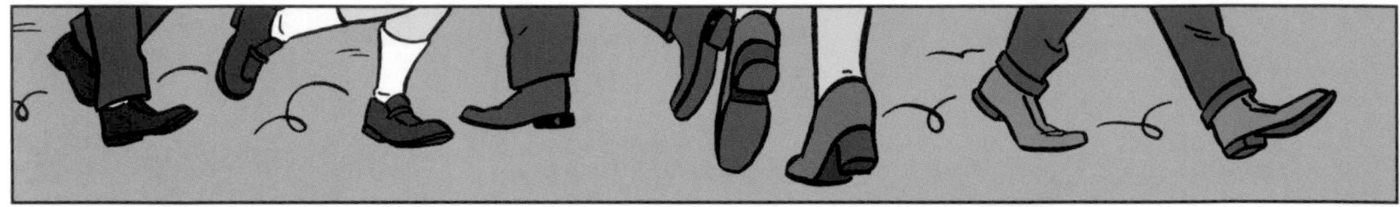

Come on!

Rats!

A5618

3RD AVE.
E. 91 ST.
ONE-WAY

3RD AVE.
E. 104 ST
ONE-WAY

YARDLY CONSTRUCTION

What's he want in there?

Went to library. Be back soon.

Ow!
POKE!

FLIP
FLIP

Code?
FISSION?

Wow... swanky. I wonder where the family went?

Rats!

What'd you do?
Nothing!

CRUMBLE!

Tony?
Help!

The dumbwaiter's got me... he wants to send me to the second floor!

Ah, ha, ha, ha, ha!
Talk about dumb.

Ha, ha, ha, ha...

?

Tony?

...sigh...

CREEAK...

CRREAK...

CRR...

!
CRACK!

CRACK!

HELP!

Yeah right... I'm not fallin' for that! Quit kiddin' around already!

WRIGGLE, WRIGGLE!

rrr...

I'm upstairs!
Check!

HARRIS
RELOCATION
VRR...

HARRIS

KREEEEEAK...

CREAK...

CREEAK...

CREEAK...

CREEEAK...

YANK!
RRR...
RUMBLE...

CREEAK...
HARRIS

RUMBLE...

CREEAK...

CLUNK!

CREEAK...
HARRIS

RATTLE!

CREEAK...

RUMBLE...

HARRIS

CREEAK

CREEAK
HARRIS

HOP!

CLUNK!

HARRIS

AAH... ACHOO!

SLAM!
He's gone!

HARRIS

There!

703
HARRIS
TAXI
SKYVIEW CAB

Follow that truck... and hurry!

Haven't you ever used a cab before? You gotta flag your own.
YANK!

Hey taxi!
HARRIS RELOCATION
P6500

ZOOOM!

PHWEEE!!!

ZOOM!
TAXI
0335P

Hold on.

Ha, ha, ha...
VROOM!

I think in the movie, she was over ten.

Well, who's going to stop for two kids?
Only someone with no pride at all.

Hey, kiddies. Need a lift?

TAXI
PUT, PUT...

19TH
PRECINC
POLICE
N.Y.

19TH
PRECI

Anyway... I didn't mean to bother you, and it's probably nothing... but I figured it might be a lead.

Although I'm afraid to say, Evelyn found it...
Great. My favorite source...

Well, you *did* say "you never know."

♪♫ Da-da-daa - dada! ♫

♪ Daaaaaaa! ♩

SWERVE!

♪ DA! ♫

SWERVE!!

Hey, Mister... would you quit it? We're gonna get killed!
Sorry! It's my chubby feet! They grow 'em big in my family!

My sister's what you call "plump," but my kid brother's more, well, "bulky"! I guess I'm "stocky."

None of us is "svelte," that's for—
Hey, Mister! Go back to singing!

Look! He's turning!

HARRIS
RELOCATION

We better get out here, so he won't see us.

Okay, kids. That'll be fourteen-fifty, American.

Well? Go ahead and pay him.
I, uh...

You mean you don't got any money? But I thought you were rich!
...usually, a grownup handles the money part...

But isn't that really expensive?
It cost a lot, but that doesn't mean it's worth much.

What'd he do... disappear?
I don't know. Hey... you smell something?

KRR...

BRRIIINNGGG!!

Now!
BRIINNG!

BBRIINNG!!
KRR...

Nein... I haven't... not yet. I'll hold off then. But— here? When?
KRR...

Ach... okay, then...

Sigh...
HAR
CLICK!

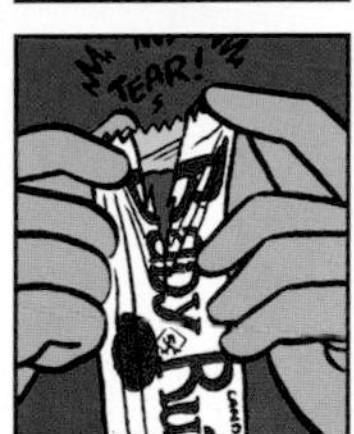
TEAR!

CRUNCH, CRUNCH!
HARRIS

VROOM...

CREEAK...

So they said you were coming. Vat is the problem?
HAR

You know vat the problem is.
I don't. This is all news to me.

Don't play around, Mueller. We know what you've been up to. And don't think it's going to mean anything.
FLICK!

Ve'll just go to Plan 2, that's all. So the joke's on you.

Look, you're making a big mistake here, I—

CRUSH!

BLAM!

SLAM!

VRRMMMMM...

I'm gonna be sick
I'm gonna be sick...

We've got to do something.
I'm gonna be sick...

th-

Don't talk, Mister. We'll get you some help...

Jimmy's in the... gingerbread house.

kk-

SHHHHHHH...

Tony... are you okay?

Then why'd you wanna go gimme a heart attack for!
CUFF!

Evelyn... where were you? You can't just take off like that, I—

... I'm sorry. Yes?

The ride cost twelve bags of potatoes.
...oh.

So that's it? You're not going to tell me what happened?

I have an idea. How about you and I go catch a poetry reading?

SLUMP...

I have a better idea. How about we go into the kitchen and make some butterscotch brownies?

So, kid... I can't make this a long one. What's up?

I don't know if this is gonna mean anything... but I thought you might be interested in this.

You see the headlines?
TAP
TAP
The Daily Gazette
MYSTERY CABIN MURDER

You mean the guy killed upstate? They said it was a robbery.
That's what we want you to think. He was one of ours.
The Daily Gazett
MYSTERY CABIN MURDER

You mean... he was a double agent?
Mueller was one of the best. He was acting as point man for the Nazi cell in the Northeast...

Until those bastards got wise to him.
But I don't get it. Point man? How did it work?

He'd wire us stuff like this as soon as the spies got it to him.

We'd doctor it so it was useless before he sent it on to Germany.
But what is it?

The plans for the most **top-secret** weapon the US is developing in this war. It's so **hush-hush** they won't even tell me the details. **Now with Mueller dead**, we think they're gonna try to get the info out of the country some **other way**. **Radar, submarines.** They even have this new technology... **micro-photography**, they call it.

ICES
SODAS · ICE CREAM · SUNDAES ·
Well, that's an interesting choice. I guess if I had to choose... I'd rather be able to fly.
But wouldn't you wanna be able to turn invisible? That way, you'd know what all your enemies were saying behind your back.
Come in We're OPEN

Good point. Plus you'd be able to get into movies for free. I—
KNOCK, KNOCK!

Hey... look who's there!
Oh brotherrr.
TAP, TAP!

So. You like mysteries, don't you, Evelyn?
I told you... we thought it was a bomb. We didn't know the doorman had a lady friend!

What? Ohh... forget that, that's ancient history. But your aunt showed me some interesting papers you found, and...

I told you... I don't want to talk about it!

Come in We're OPEN

Evelyn? Evelyn — come back!

Lechah dodi, likrat kalah
penei shabat nekabelah
?

Shamor vezachor bedibur echad hishmi'anu el hameyuchad, hashem echad ushmo echad leshem uletiferet velitehilah, Lechah dodi...

Lechah dodi
That's a whatchamacallit, right? The thing in my mom's wedding picture.

The chuppah. Yes. It's a bridal canopy.
Is this a church?
Kind of.

Hey Aunt Lia? We're Jews, right?
Yes, of course we are. Why do you ask?

It's just that... we never do anything about it.
Maybe not. But it's what we are. You should be proud of it.

Mazel tov!
KRSSH!

...but we're Americans, too.
Thank heavens. God only knows what's happening to those poor Jews over in Europe.

You mean because of Hitler? He hates the Jews?
He hates a lot of people, honey. But yes—he really hates the Jews.

And is that why we're fighting?
Yeah, kid, I guess you could say that.

Officer?
SNIFF

Hey, Officer Hughes?
TUG TUG

THOOM!
Hey!
Oh, no!
DANGER! STREET CLOSED FOR BUILDING DEMOLITION
YARDLY
F5273
SCREECH!!!
THOOM!

It was right over here... we're almost there...

My brother said they'd be in a hurry once they knew we were on to them.

Well... I bet Tony and me could recognize the guy with the book. Or at least Tony could. Or...

Maybe he left his fingerprints somewhere, and if we could find 'em, we could...

It's getting late.

YANKEE DOODLE
PASTRY SHOP
Sorry WE'RE CLOSED
NOTICE TO CUSTOMERS:

Figures. We can't even get a cup of coffee.
"We kneaded a little rest... so have gone to bake in the sun."
Hey that's pretty good. Get it? "Kneaded" a little rest?

That's funny. They were open just this morning.

Hansel and Gretel...

Yeah... you're right. This place wasn't always called Yankee Doodle. It used to have a different name...

Wait a second... it sure did...

THE GINGERBREAD HOUSE

I've got to call my brother pronto. Stay here and keep your eyes peeled.

J&J HATS
I sure hope Mrs. Schmidt is okay. You think the Nazis got to her?
PASTRY SHOP

Hey, Evelyn... look!

Evelyn?

Yankee Doodle
Pastry Shop

Gut... One more trip should do it...

Holy kamoley...!

Cheese it, Evelyn... they're coming!
Quick... get in!

CLUNK, CLUNK

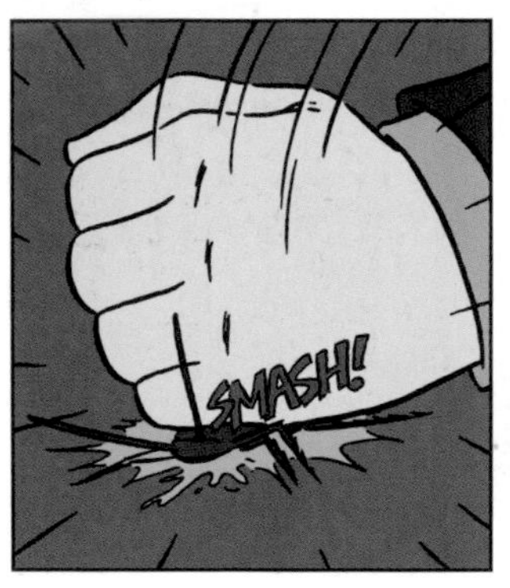
SMASH!

Yecch. Cockroach!
WIPE, WIPE

SLAM!

Alles okay?
Ja. All set.

VRRMM!

PHONE
TELEPHONE
AME
TAIL

Where'd they go?
BOOKS
J&J HATS
J&J
HATS
F5273

PASTRY SHOP
YANKEE DOODLE
PASTRY SHOP
VRRM!

COUGH... COUGH... SPUTTER...
F5273

Quick... let's take my limo!

How is the time?

Don't worry. We're fine.

GURGLE

You'd better not... they'll notice!

GURGLE...

Just think of something really disgusting. Liver and onions... old smelly mackerels...

GURGLE!

Perhaps ve should have eaten before ve left?
Ja... Perhaps...

Head cheese... Brussel sprouts... my grandma's chest when she hugs me hello...

Which way?
Umm... let's try that turn!

YANKEE DOODLE PASTRY SHOP
ERRRTT..
I'll take this. You can bring the rest in later.
CLANG!
C'mon.

BARK! BARK! BARK! BARK!
Aah-!
Eek!

Grrr...

BARK! BARK!

Poor Queenie. Hungry for some of that cake?
Whine...

You come inside with me and I'll see if I can't rustle up some treats for you.

Phew!

Why, look... two little children. How unexpected.

HA
HA
YAAH!
HA
HA
HA

Hey—who are *they*?

Did anyone invite 'em?
'Cause I sure as heck didn't.

I did.

They're my friends, okay?

I think we saw a movie together once.
WINK!

Do you think Jimmy's here?
SHRUG...

Well, well. If it isn't our *guter Freund*, "Dr. Johnson."

Or vas it "Smith" or "Jones"?
Whichever. God bless America.
I'll drink to that. And thank your relatives for the excellent cover, too... Cute!

I think you're all relaxing a little early.
Why? Liesel's got it all under control.

Her job isn't over. She still has to get the plans to our men onboard that liner. Then the plans have to be smuggled to Berlin... so many things can go wrong...

What a worrier. Drink up!
...sigh...

Oh... well, maybe a short one...

Hurrah!
Here's to bumping off Uncle Sam... with his own gun. *Heil Hitler!*

Heil Hitler!
CLINK!
CLINK!
CLINK!

Any idea where they went?
Not really. But I got a hunch they headed for the water... that's where the serious money is.

Okay, kids! Watch out!

WONK!

You stink!

Yeah! Bring on the dancing girls!
Please... children! Settle down!
BOO!
HISS!

Now who wants to play a nice game of "Pin the Tail on the Donkey"?
Yeah, Harold... stick a pin in your keister!

Wait! Doesn't anyone want to play a nice game?
HA
HA
HA
HA
HA

SPIN!

KISS...

...sigh...

KISS!

Excuse me... is there a Jimmy here?
SHUT THAT DOOR!

KISS!

?
CLUNK!

RATTLE!

KISS!

CLUNK!

Whoo. That was close.

Yeah... that was a great idea.

Kids... get out here! We've got a big surprise for you!

C'mon... we'd better check it out.

DASH!

Okay, kids—it's that time!
HONK HONK!

BOOT!

Why ya little—
Ahem! It's time to celebrate what we're all here for—
HA!
HA!
HA!
HA!
HA!

Harold's twelfth birthday!
BOO!

And how do we do that? Why, with a delicious cake!

HONK
HONK
Happy Birthday Harold!

Hey... what gives?
That's not the cake from the truck!

CAKE!
YA!
OOH!

SHLURP! NNUM!
GULP!

Böser Hund! Böser Hund! Du elendes Biest!
Urf!?
WACK!
YANK!

Josef! Get it back!
What?! How do I do that... ?

Get him to sick it up! Use your fingers! What's the matter, haven't you ever done that to anyone?
Well—uh, no, I—

Ach! All right, I'll help you... kommen Sie auf!

SLAM!
Did you see that? Something's gotta be in the cake!

So c'mon... dig in.

GOOSH!

What are we looking for?
Beats me.

BLURF!
Good! Good! That's it!
Well, now what do we do?

What do you think? Get the jimmies! Pick them out of the sick!
... the jimmies?!

You mean the sprinkles?

Well, look who's here...

YANKEE DOODLE
PASTRY SHOP

HA
HA
HA

You look down that way and I'll check this end.

We know what you've been doing! You're Nazi spies, and there's something in the jimmies, and—
Tony, hush up!

Hmm!

GLINT!
GLEAM!

You know these two?
I know they like hot apple pie with ice cream on top.
WIPE, WIPE

Don't you, dear?

So—you figured everything out. Pretty clever, aren't you?

Who else did you tell?

...No one. It's just us.

I see...

So, Liebchen... what is your name?

Evelyn. Evelyn Weiss... And I think you should know my father's rich and he has a lot of important friends, so—

Shut your mouth!

"Weiss." So you're a little German girl, is that right?
She's Jewish, you idiot!

Shush, you!

Look! — there's someone at the door!

ESCAPE!

EEK!

SLAP!

WHUMP!
Help! Hel-mmph!

I think this one needs to be taught a lesson. Perhaps she needs to come back with us—

They should have started out by now. Stupid woman.

Don't mind this one... you know how they are at this age, Mr. Weiss...

... a bunch of wild Indians!
That's for sure! But what do you say we let him roam the prairie now, okay?
PAT, PAT

...strudel and coffee wasn't it? Just like all the other...

...cops.

BAM!

EEEEEEEEK!

Raar!
Ahh! Ha, ha, ha, ha!

SNEAK...

Eep!

Er... Hi.
Hi.

You looking for your friend?

Quick... they're expecting us!

Hmph!

Gasp!

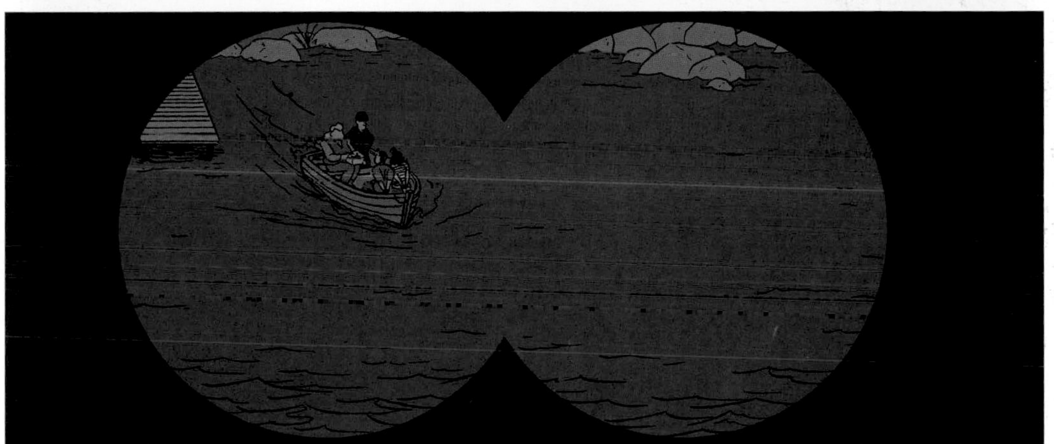

Finally... that stupid cow!

SPLASH!

Slow down, for God's sake!
We're late as it is!

And what about those two? I say ve push them in and have it done with.
Don't be stupid. Why get our hands dirty?

Leave it to them... They will know how to handle it...

No. Tell him it's his brother, and it's an emergency!

FLIP, FLIP

Pat? Look. Don't ask questions, just get yourself and your boys out to the Island, pronto. 70 Cliff Hook Drive, Brightwater.

And yes it *is* serious - but only if you want to win the war!

... Brendan?

You might want to call your brother back.

It was hard enough calling him the first time.

TOSS!
WAM!

GRAPPLE!

BANG!

Oh, Brendan...

KISS!

Are you okay?
Yeah.

Then let's go.

mmmm...
Ach!—Let's undo that one, she's giving me a headache!

RIP!

?

Excess baggage. Will you deal with it later?

Fine—just give me the damned cake.

I hope I will be properly compensated for my efforts.
Yes, yes. Hand it over.
TUG!

So? What will I get?

POW!

POW!

Hey Tony? Think the Dodgers have a shot at the pennant?

... the Dodgers...?

POW!
PHUT!

PHWEE!

WRIGGLE!
SLIP!

Watch out!
RIP!

POW!
POW!
Aghk!
SPLISH!

Scheiss!

The cake!
Let's just get outta here!
WHIZZZ!
SPLISH!

Good evening.
Er!—Good evening.
HIDE!
VRRM

You know how to start this thing?
Sure... I'm good at fixing things, remember?
VRRM!

Lovely night.
...just lovely.
VRRM!

VRRM-RRRR-RRRR!

VIZZZ!
EEK!
ZOOOM!
SPLISH!

We've got to stop it!

YANK!

TWANG!

JUMP!

Hey... over here!

Evelyn!

WEEE
OOO
WEEE
OOOO
WEEE
OOO

Thanks for the call.
That's what they pay me for.

Yeah, it is now, Bren... It is now...

They were the plans for the weapon, all right—shrunk down to the size of grains of sand. They were embedded in wax so they'd look like chocolate jimmies.
Cute... Will I ever know what it was?

Maybe one day we'll all know. It's some kind of bomb.

Hey. Come over for dinner next week?
Okay. But this time, set a plate for Amelia Earhart.

Well, you may not have saved the cake... but you sure saved our bacon.
Really?

Hey, speaking of bacon... do you think we could stop someplace and get something to eat? We're *starving*.
Yeah. We didn't even get any of that cake!

And thanks to you two, it looks like the Nazis won't, either.

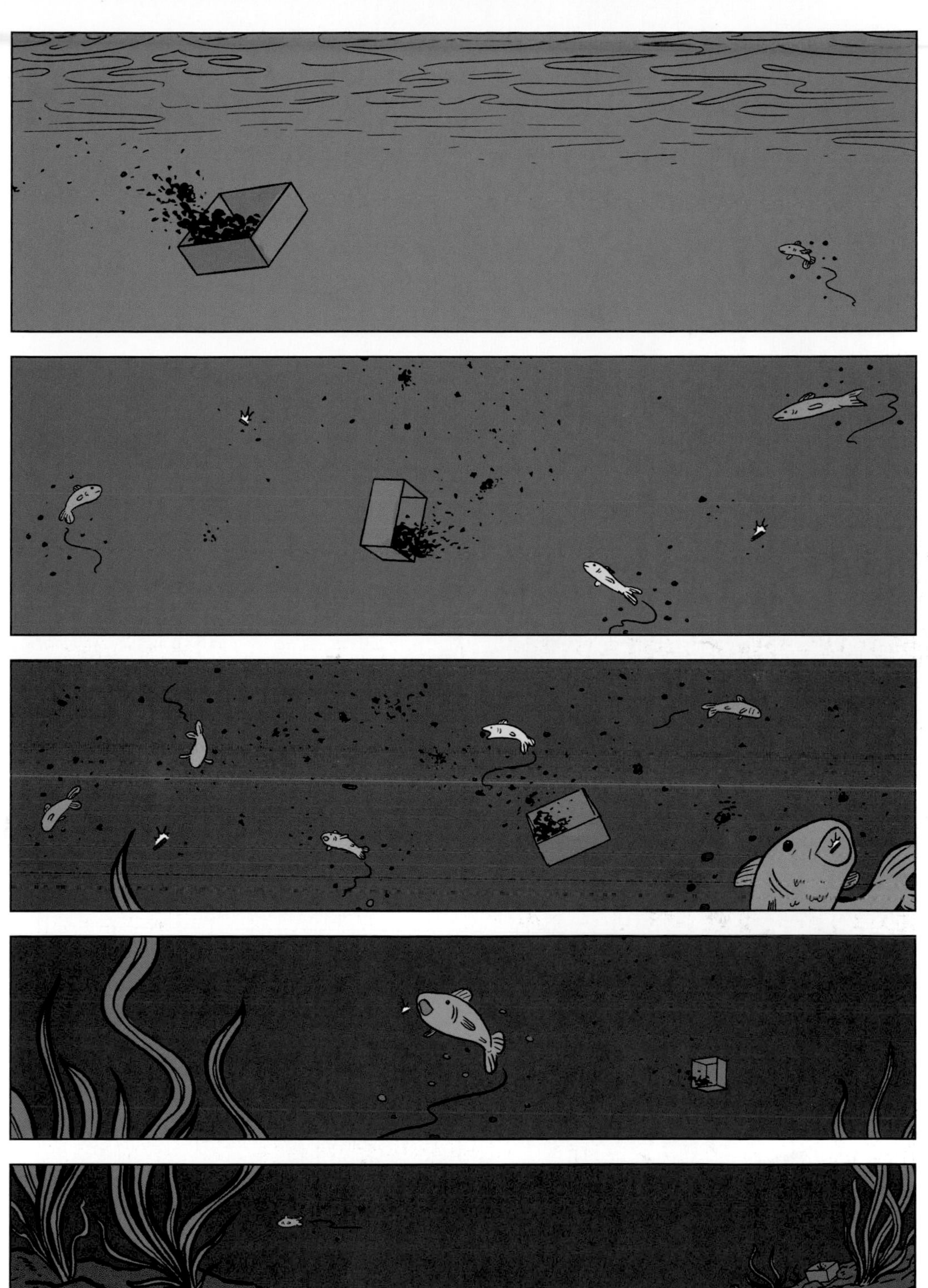

Seven weeks later
NO PARKING

Here... This one's for you.
Cracker Jack
PRIZE

Oh no...!

I'm sorry, Evelyn... but your dad's car is on its way.

But I thought I still had all afternoon!

Oh...

It's only Connecticut, you know...
And you promise I can come visit anytime I want? Cross your heart and hope to die?
Cross my heart and hope to die.

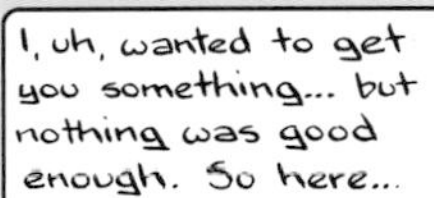

I, uh, wanted to get you something... but nothing was good enough. So here...

I guess I won't need it, since they made me detective. And I can't think of anyone who deserves it more.

HUG!

Hey, Tony, look wha...

Tony...?

I gotta fix this... thingamajig before it... fritzes out again...
CLONG!
CLONG!

You aren't ever comin' back, are you?
Of course I am!

No you won't. You'll be making new friends at your fancy-pants school and you won't ever think about me, and we'll never have any more adventures!
CLONG!
CLONG! CLONG!
CLONG!

Oh yeah?... Well, didn't you hear what happened to the Hope diamond?
...What about it?

Nothing. Only it's been stolen.

For real?

They say it's genuine. But don't you think they coulda switched it for a fake one made of glass...?

CLUNK!

Goodbye! See you soon! Goodbye!

SLUMP...

Sigh...

?
Greetings

Jack? Do you have a matchbook I could borrow?
Matchbook? You ain't takin' up smoking, are ya?

Nope. I'll give it right back.

PLANT YOU NOW, DIG YOU LATER!

GIRL ARCHAEOLOGIST EVELYN WEISS AND INTREPID EXPLORER TONY VITUCCI WERE IN SEARCH OF TREASURE!

THEY WERE SEEKING THE ANCIENT STATUE OF THE GREAT JUNGLE GOD XOCOLATYL...

—THAT IT WAS, IN FACT, THE LEGENDARY HOPE DIAMOND!
C'MON!
STEP!
LOOK OUT!
SHEW!
PLEASE BE CAREFUL!!
A DOOR!
IT LOOKS SCARY